Ebenezer Bowman

Alphabets of Intemperance

fifteen direct shots at the upas tree of intemperance, or the temperance

argument in a nut shell

Ebenezer Bowman

Alphabets of Intemperance
fifteen direct shots at the upas tree of intemperance, or the temperance argument in a nut shell

ISBN/EAN: 9783337390181

Printed in Europe, USA, Canada, Australia, Japan

Cover: Foto ©Andreas Hilbeck / pixelio.de

More available books at **www.hansebooks.com**

———•———

FIFTEEN DIRECT SHOTS

AT

THE UPAS TREE

OF

INTEMPERANCE,

OR THE

TEMPERANCE ARGUMENT

IN A NUT SHELL.

BY EBENEZER BOWMAN.

———•———

TOTAL ABSTINENCE ROOMS,
36 BROMFIELD STREET, BOSTON, MASS.,
Room 3.

PREFACE.

It is said that a gentleman and his son, aged respectively ninety and sixty years, went together to a piece of woods to test the comparative accuracy of their marksmanship, and commenced the exercise by firing at a squirrel in the top of a tall tree. The younger of the two fired several shots, but his squirrelship still held his position with a provoking smile. At last the elder, who was shaking badly with palsy, succeeded in getting the son to let him try his hand at the business.

He aimed the gun, which it was impossible for his aged hand to direct with steadiness ; his eye ran quickly along the barrel, at the right instant he fired ; the squirrel fell quickly at his feet with a streak of daylight shining through his head, when he exultingly turned to the young lad of sixty and exclaimed : "Didn't I tell you I could fetch him." Whereat the youngster, · very crestfallen, and scarcely looking up, retorted : "Well, I should think you'd ought to hit him ; you fired all over the tree."

The only apology that the author of these *Alphabets of Intemperance* has the time, or the desire, to offer, is that it is the humble effort of one who has felt an intense interest in the fight against the "drink demon" since early boyhood to aim a volley of shot at the monster in such a manner as, if possible, to "fire all over the tree."—E. B.

A for Alcohol, man's deadliest foe ;
  It poisons his brain, and brings him down low ;
  It ruins his soul, his reason destroys,
  It changes to Sots our loveliest boys.

B is for Bondage, of body and soul,
  For those who submit to liquor's control,
  From Tippler, to Sot, the path is so plain,
  Those only are safe who always abstain.

C for Carousals, where liquor flows free,
  Where morals are loose, and all are in glee ;
  Where conscience is drowned, or driven away,
  Where children of sin their father obey.

D for Dram-Seller, who seeking his gains,
  Ruins his neighbors in pocket and brains ;
  Sickness and sorrow he spreads far around,
  And causes disgrace to widely abound.

E for Example, which Christians should live,
  So holy, and pure, as none to deceive,
  Avoiding the cup that leads down to hell,
  Where drunkards are doomed in darkness to dwell.

F for the Folly of thoughtless young men,
  Who tamper with wine again, and again,
  Their will growing weak, beyond their control,
  Till all is destroyed, of body and soul.

G is for Gladness, which liquor repels,
  From homes of delight, where happiness dwells.
  How many bright hopes, and innocent joys,
  This cup of deceit, now daily destroys.

H is for Heaven, where holy and pure,
  Redeemed ones of earth from sin are secure,
  No drunkard is there, to mar the bright scene :
  There holiness reigns ; there none are unclean.

I for Idleness, the cause of much sin,
  Where vices, and crimes, so often steal in,
  Innocence, seldom with idlers is found,
  While drunkenness, there is sure to abound.

J is for Judgment—in which all must stand
  Who favor this traffic ; throughout every land,
  Judgment, and Justice, will seal their black doom,
  Unless, ere too late, repentance shall come.

K is for Kingdom of heavenly grace,
  Where all are redeemed from sin's vile embrace ;
  Its worst foe is Rum, the Devil's Right Bower,
  Which holds men in sin, with absolute power.

L is for Lucre, which tempts men to sin ;
  Its power is so great o'er millions of men,
  That conscience, no more rules over the soul,
  But leaves it a slave in Satan's control.

M is for Mother—heart broken and sad,
  Because her dear boy has proven so bad ;
  That once lovely child o'er which her heart yearned,
  By sipping the wine, a drunkard has turned.

N was the Neglect, in childhood's bright days
  To teach her dear boy, sobriety's ways,
  If taught when a child the wine cup to shun,
  This path of deceit, had ne'er been begun.

O is for Owners of Real Estate,
  Who serve the devil, both early, and late,
  Renting their buildings to servants of sin,
  Ruining homes, with Beer, Brandy, and Gin.

P is for Preaching, and Practice, combined,
The mightiest power we ever shall find,
To drive the demon of drink far away,
And make our homes, safe from Alcohol's sway.

Q for Quintessence of vileness of speech,
To which the users of liquor may reach,
Blaspheming their God, degrading their soul,
Submitting their lives to Satan's control.

R for redemption, the Almighty power
Which God gave to man in Calvary's hour,
In Jesus believe—the Devil resist,
From you he will flee, your life will be blessed.

S is for sadness, for sorrow and sin,
Which tippling creates; Oh! do not begin,
But take the life pledge, and always abstain.
Not ever, to taste the poison again.

T for Transgressor, now in the *hard road*,
O'erburdened with sin, a wearisome load ;
Drink all remorseless, now binds him in chains,
His conscience a slave—lust holding the reins.

U for Ugliness, which liquor brings out,
And puts it to work, without any doubt ;
It strengthens the man to shoot, stab, or kill,
Guided by Satan, he follows his will.

V is for voter, who knowing his might,
His ballot should cast for reason, and right,
When voters, decide this ruin shall cease,
In homes of despair, we soon will have peace.

W for Wisdom, whose teachings divine,
Forbid us to look on fermented wine,
Though pleasant at first, we're told it will bring
At the last, the Adder's venomous sting.

X stands for cross, the comfort and hope
　　Of all who believe—to that we'll look up ;
　　But faith without works, possesses no power,
　　While both, when combined, bring victory's hour.

Y is for the Young, for them we'll contend,
　　On whom our country so soon must depend ;
　　If they keep the pledge with honor through life,
　　We soon will be free from drink's deadly strife.

Z is for Zeal, which all should possess,
　　Who sympathy feel, for other's distress,
　　May all be imbued with zeal for this cause,
　　Which brings us to live by nature's just laws.

& let us all, *work*—while the day lasts,
　　For night cometh soon, when *work* will be past ;
　　So work for the Right ; *Work, work*, while we may,
　　And God in his might, will speed the glad day.

SHOT No. 2.

A the Appetite, for brandy and gin,
 Produces disease, encourages sin.

B for the Beer, which sharpens the taste,
 Then whisky, and gin, increase the disgrace.

C is for Cider, which kindles the fire
 Of appetite fierce, which brandy fans higher.

D for the Devil; he's always well pleased
 To witness this work, in all the degrees.

E for Express, the tippler's *quick train*,
 That take's him through drink to satan's domain.

F for the Folly of *tasting at all*,
 When many, by tasting, receive such a fall.

G is for Goodness, to which *none will rise*,
 Who follow through drink the father of lies.

H is for Hardness, of heart and of life,
 Which drink brings to homes, with sorrow and strife.

I the Innocents, whose parents through drink,
 Cause them deep in shame and sorrow to sink.

J is for Jug, with infamy filled,
 It poison contains, both brewed and distilled.

K is for King, to no other we'll bend,
 Than Jesus, our Lord, our brother, and friend.

L is for Landlord, whose conscience is gone—-
 For money ; he lets this business go on.

M for the Masses, the might *they possess*
To banish this curse, humanity bless.

N for Narcotic, which, taken in health,
Confuses our brain, reduces our wealth.

O is for Order, which drinking destroys,
With all of our hopes of heavenly joys.

P for Pollution, the state of the soul,
When poisoned by drink, in *satan's control.*

Q is for Quarrels created by wine,
Which good men *always*, should *promptly decline.*

R for Redemption, through Jesus' blood,
Which *cleanses from sin*, and *brings us to God.*

S says we must Shun drink's wretched embrace
By signing the pledge, thus shunning disgrace.

T for Transgressor, *his way, oh ! how hard !*
Which way would be smooth, if truth he'd regard.

U is for Union, to save men from drink,
Which many doth cause in darkness to sink.

V is for Vices, begotten by wine,
This poisonous cup, pray always decline.

W is for Wisdom, to which all should turn,
This cup of deceit forever to spurn.

X stands for cross—our Savior died there,
That all who believe, his mansions may share.

Y is for Youth, when all should embrace,
The pledge against drink, and seek for true grace.

Z is for Zeal, which *all* should inspire,
Who, working for truth, raise humanity higher.

& may we all work, still trusting in God—
Proclaiming these truths forever abroad.

SHOT No. 3.

A is for Ale-house, where people hang round,
    Whose brains are diseased, whose minds are unsound,
    Where many lessons in vice, crime and sin,
    In ways of deceit are sure to begin.

B stands for the Boy who scorns good advice,
    Who frequents such shops, and thinks it quite nice;
    Who fears not to sip the poisonous drink,
    Who starts to despair, not stopping to think.

C is for Causes that lead us away
    From virtue and peace, to wander astray—
    More go down to death through beer, gin, and wine,
    Than all other causes that ever combine.

D is for Deceit, Destruction, Despair,
    Which often we meet where all appears fair,
    And for Delusion o'er body and soul,
    That lurks in the cup, the glass, or the bowl.

E is for Ease with which people go down
    To ruin's abyss, with wine bibbers found,
    The path strewn with flowers, they enter at first,
    With thistles and thorns is speedily cursed.

F stands for Fiends, who merrily dance,
    As outward they look o'er sin's broad expanse,
    And see men beguiled by wine's glitter and glow,
    With them to endure the kingdom of woe.

G is for Gospel, which never can spread,
    And bring souls to life in trespasses dead,
    O'er whom the red wine holds terrible sway,
    'Till this *mocker* of souls is driven away.

H is for our Homes, where all should agree
 From drinks that destroy to ever be free—
 Which, happy and bright, where abstinence dwells,
 Through wine's *fearful blight* are changed into hells.

I is for Idler, inducements are strong
 For him to enlist in drink's ragged throng;
 More recruits to perdition, from his ranks are received
 Than from all other sources, 'tis firmly believed.

J is for Jail, a station house fine,
 For all who travel the " Black Valley " line;
 Get tickets at dram shops, when ready to go,
 Refresh at these stations where prices are low.

K is for Kingdom where infamy reigns,
 Whose subjects are black with sin's guilty stains.
 The *prince of narcotics* there stands at the helm,
 And with grasp quite satanic rules those in his realm.

L is for Law, may the standard be high,
 To remove from the *weak*, temptations that try;
 That *less snares* may infest the highway of life
 To allure unto death through sorrow and strife.

M is for Means that satan employs,
 To entice into sin our girls and our boys;
 He *laughs*, when the wine flows social and free,
 When souls are destroyed, he capers with glee.

N is for Need of heroes sublime,
 To scatter the truth throughout every clime;
 Who quail not at satire, though pointed and keen,
 And feel a true loathing for everything mean.

O is for Obtuse, the state of the brain,
 That muddled by drink can see nothing plain;
 Not wanted below, above it repairs,
 The skull holds it close, a prisoner there.

P is the Prisoner; confined in this cell
  He starts a disturbance, and causes a spell
  To come o'er his guards, and hold them at bay,
  While he slyly sneaks out and scampers away.

Q is for Quarrels, which often arise,
  When the brain *thus diseased*, acts very unwise;
  The man, thus deluded, takes a friend for a foe,
  Strikes out for his rights, and is quickly laid low.

R is for Ruin, that lurks at each step,
  Of *all who continue this poison to sip*.
  There's danger to all who tamper with drink,
  They travel 'mong pitfalls where many must sink.

S is for Serpent, which hidden from view,
  Is lurking in wine for each jolly crew;
  He darts out his fangs when looked for the least,
  And *stings unto death*, both people and priest.

T is for Thief; to liquor applied
  It steals man's good sense, his reason, his pride;
  It robs him of home, of virtue and friends,
  And sends him, to dwell 'mong demons and fiends.

U is for Union, which should ever prevail
  'Mong those enlisted the wrong to assail;
  And for Useless, which applies with much force
  To all who *grumble*, as a matter of course.

V is for Value, which all should agree
  Pertains to the pledge, from drink to be free,
  For *thus we enlist*, to fight 'gainst the foe,
  That brings to our homes, such sorrow and woe.

W, for Want, which many endure,
  Who, cursed by the cup, too often are sure
  To go to ruin with hazardous speed,
  Sound teachings of Wisdom still failing to heed.

X stands for Cross, on Calvary placed
    From sin to redeem ; *to save* a *lost race ;*
    If to that we'll cling, temptations to death
    Will quickly turn round, and flee from our path.

Y is for Yearnings of wisdom and love,
    That lift us from sin, direct us above ;
    May we yearn to love the good and the true,
    And follow our journey in happiness through.

Z is for Zeal, which should ever imbue,
    With earnest intent the good and the true ;
    And make us stand firm when dangers surround,
    With grace and good works to always abound.

& now may we all from liquors refrain,
    Which have cursed our race, again and again ;
    But drink pure water, so sparkling and bright,
    Be earnest tee-totlars, and live for the right.

Shot No. 4.

A for the Appetite the drunkard possesses,
　　It fills him with pains, with woes and distresses;
　　It binds him in chains and sends him to prison,
　　Diseases his body, unsettles his reason.

B is for Bondage sad hearts are enduring,
　　Because of the drink, enticing, alluring;
　　This bondage above all others is galling,
　　The bodies and souls of drinkers enthralling.

C is for Conscience, no longer disturbing
　　The soul of the sot, his infamy curbing;
　　His conscience he's drowned, instead of his sorrow,
　　All darkness to day, no hope for the morrow.

D for Delusion, the soul's sad condition,
　　Of peace and content, in sight of perdition;
　　May God's holy truth these victims awaken,
　　'Till the kingdom of woe is thoroughly shaken.

E is for Effort this bondage to sever,
　　By practice, by preaching and pledges forever;
　　All these we will use, while a tippler remaining,
　　Endangers his soul, this practice sustaining.

F for False Friends, by whom men are guided,
　　Whose *better* natures, would make them decided
　　To leave the vile drink, to them so debasing,
　　And thus, the bright path of virtue, retracing.

G the Gratitude, drunkards' wives are all feeling,
　　That christians are now to their husbands appealing,
　　To break from their bonds of sin and delusion,
　　And rescue their homes from endless confusion.

H is for Heart-aches, so deeply distressing,
　The woe sinks below the power of guessing ;
　All brought about by this custom of drinking,
　Which custom to death, its victims is sinking.

I the Impenitent, still drinking, carousing,
　The cause of all vileness, intensely espousing,
　Their children and wives, how sadly disgracing,
　Their manhood and honor completely effacing.

J for the Journey so swifty they're speeding,
　Sound teachings of truth so surely unheeding ;
　They pass down to woe, through riots, and revels,
　To make their abode in darkness, with devils.

K is for Keepers of vile drinking places,
　Whose every day life, true manhood disgraces ;
　May public opinion, in *tidal waves rising*,
　Destroy their vile trade in a manner surprising.

L is for License this traffic assisting,
　To murder by law, wives' pleadings resisting,
　Licensed, these dealers *all heaven defying*,
　Their coffers may fill, 'mong wounded and **dying**.

M is for Mourners o'er burdened with sorrow,
　Heart-broken to-day, hope gone for the morrow—
　That nearest of friends, all reason ignoring,
　Are sunk in disgrace past heaven's restoring.

N for the Neglected children of sorrow,
　Filling *our alleys to-day, our prisons to-morrow*.
　When christians unite this traffic to banish,
　These waifs of neglect will speedily vanish.

O the Opposition beyond all resisting,
　Which christians should make, all virtue assisting,
　Opposing through life, the custom, and traffic,
　Which makes with our race such terrible havoc.

P for the Pledge—the bond for uniting
  Our army of truth, this enemy fighting;
  It makes us secure from drink's desolation,
  And should be extended throughout every nation.

Q for this Question, which all should endeavor
  To settle aright—and settle forever;
  When settled with sense, from liquors abstaining,
  Our race will be sober, no drunkard remaining.

R for the Resources all nations are losing,
  Whose people with drink their brains are confusing,
  God's grain, made for food, they're rotting, distilling,
  Bright homes, far and near, with infamy filling.

S songs to Jehovah, abstainers are raising,
  Freed from appetite's bonds their God they're praising;
  That drink's galling chains no longer are binding,
  Their natures polluting, their consciences blinding.

T is for Truth, which aimed with precision,
  May sinners induce to make the decision,
  To flee from a life of sin, shame, and sadness,
  And scale the bright heights, of triumph and gladness

U the Undying warfare we are waging
  To banish the curse of liquor so raging;
  The bodies, and souls, of many destroying,
  No happiness here, or hereafter, enjoying.

V is for Value of law, love, and reason,
  The triune of power to banish this treason
  Against all the laws that govern our nature,
  Defying Jehovah, defiling the creature.

W the Wisdom with which we're fighting
  To banish this custom and traffic uniting,
  For dealer, and victim, we'll use moral suasion,
  With *good law* behind us, for needed occasion.

X the eXample true parents are giving,
  Their children to teach, the right way of living;
  Example, and precept, for temperance uniting,
  So potent for good, too many are slighting.

Y for the Young—so tender, confiding,
  Their course for all time, they now are deciding,
  If teachings of truth, in their minds are implanted,
  They'll hold them through life, with courage undaunted.

Z is for Zeal of the masses uprising,
  Spreading the truth in a manner surprising;
  When christians unite to fight against evil,
  Redeemed human nature, shall conquer the devil.

& now one and all—our trust in Jehovah,
  These truths, we will teach the wide world all over;
  'Till all of our race, from liquors abstaining
  Are freed from this curse; *no tippler remaining.*

SHOT No. 5.

A is for Adder, that lurks in the wine,
B for the Bibber, who thinks it so fine,
C for this Cup of Poison well filled,
D for the Dram of " Delusion distilled."

E is for Effort, the pledge to extend,
F for the Foolish, who'll ne'er try to mend,
G is for Gutter where drunkards recline ;
H is for Heart-aches created by wine.

I for Inn, where *loose* habits are started,
J for Jail, to which drunkards are carted ;
K for Keepers of *vile* drinking places,
L their License which our manhood disgraces.

M for Meanness begotten by drinking,
N Narcotic, the foe of right thinking,
O for Orgies, way-marks to perdition,
P for Pollution, the drunkard's condition.

Q is for Quarrels by drink scattered wide,
R is for Reason, the Teetotaler's guide,
S Sin, Shame, Sorrow, which drink ever brings,
T for the Tears from grief's scalding springs.

U is for Ungodly dealers in drink,
V for their Victims down *infamy's brink* ;
W for Wretch near the end of his race,
X stands for Cross, which he yet may embrace.

Y is for the Young, confiding and good,
Z for the Zeal that directs them to God,
& *there* they are freed from sin's galling load.

Shot No. 6.

A is for Adder, whose poisonous sting,
    Is likened to wine by wisdom of old,
But death to the body, he only can bring,
    While wine stings to death both body and soul.

B is for Biter—that lurks in the way
    Of those who decline the wine cup to shun,
He haunts the steps of the happy, and gay,
    Who tamper with wine, however begun.

C is for Caution, which none should ignore,
    When signals sound forth, "*ho ! breakers ahead !*"
But Caution, unheeded by many before,
    Has peopled by millions the land of the dead.

D for Disgrace—which so keenly is felt
    By mothers and wives, whose husbands and sons
At Bacchus' vile altar so meanly have knelt,
    'Till his blood in their veins now ignobly runs.

E is for Enemy, in guise of a friend,
    That's tempting mankind the wrong to pursue,
Don't think him a saint, he'll make you a fiend,
    E'er you follow his path of infamy through.

F is for Facts—so stubborn, so plain,
    Which speak with such force to all who will hear;
Their warnings go forth—again, and again,
    In tones that are loud, in notes that are clear.

G is for Goal—at which all should aim,
    May it not be sordid, vulgar, or mean,
But higher than honor, than riches, or fame,
    Make our hearts pure, our consciences clean.

H is for Haunts—where the low and the vile
 Are searching for joy 'mid sorrow and woe,
Our sons they allure, our daughters beguile,
 To sink with themselves in infamy low.

I for Intemperance, most surely doth stand,
 In *all the degrees—from tippler to sot ;*
Search where you please, through all our fair land,
 No place can be found, where his victims are not.

J is for Joy—which the wine cup dispels,
 Though it promises joy to all who partake,
Other agents of woe it greatly excels,
 Causing millions of hearts with anguish to break.

K is for Knife—no one would dispense
 With a thing of such use, when handled with care,
But guided by drink, 'tis used without sense,
 For murder, for strife, for wounds, and despair.

L is for Love ; all pure and divine,
 It came from the hand of our Father above ;
But poisoned by drink, polluted by wine,
 'Tis anything else but heavenly love.

M is for Millions of people on earth,
 Who, cursed by vile drink, go down to despair;
With truth for their guide, they'd seek the new birth,
 The joys of redeemed ones forever to share.

N is for Night—with darkness o'ercast,
 When wine in his pride, high carnival holds,
Then Bacchus' foul breath with infamy blasts,
 The bodies of men, their reason and souls.

O is for Order—a law from on high,
 By Wisdom conceived in councils divine;
Intemperance causes all order to die,
 And thus it destroys our Maker's design.

P for Pollution to body and soul,
　　That lurks in the path by wine bibbers trod,
Seduced by vile drink, to satan's control,
　　They wander afar from virtue and God.

Q for Quintessence of meaness and shame,
　　To which the venders of drink will descend,
Proclaiming that they are free from all blame,
　　When souls to perdition, their traffic doth send.

R is for Reason, which, sober and clear,
　　Would banish these shops from country and town,
But muddled by wine, by whisky and beer,
　　Makes places so vile, of highest renown.

S is for Shame, for Sorrow, and Sadness,
　　Which canker the soul, and fill it with gloom
For friends, and relations, deluded to madness,
　　All speeding their way to infamy's tomb.

T for Temptation, enchanting, alluring,
　　Enticing the weak, the wrong to pursue;
The souls of the good too often securing,
　　By making the false appear like the true.

U stands for Ungodly drunkards and sots,
　　Who once were as pure, as lovely, and fair,
As any dear babes in mansions or cots,
　　Protected by parents' devotion and care.

V is for Vote, which should always protect
　　The weak from the snares that compass them 'round,
That all may in truth be led to expect
　　Our laws to be based on principles sound.

W for Wisdom, whose teachings divine
　　Doth cause us the first temptation to spurn,
Thus pure in our lives, abstaining from wine,
　　Our souls, for the good, forever will burn.

X for eXertion—our race to improve,
    When dangers exist, the signal to sound ;
  Exertions, inspired by our God, must remove
    The dangers which 'round us so thickly abound.

Y is for Youth—the season to sow
    Good seed from on high deep down in the heart;
  There nourished, t'will flourish to fruitage, and grow,
    Delusions will vanish, temptations depart.

Z is for Zeal—our souls should abound
    With zeal all aglow, with faith, hope, and love,
  In works of reform, to ever be found,
    Alarming *from* sin, directing above.

& Thus, my dear friends, our lives should be passed
    In acts of devotion our race to improve,
  'Till called by our Master up higher at last,
    With him to enjoy the fruition of love.

Shot No. 7.

A for Appetite begotten by drinking,
B for the Boy that tipples unthinking ;
C for the Curse that tippling produces,
D for the Dram for drunkard's vile uses.

E for the Effort abstainers are making,
F for the Foolish, their drams still partaking,
G for Gutter whither drinkers are tending,
H for the Homes, true hearts are defending.

I is for Increase, the law of narcotics,
J is for Jim-jams, no drunkard's exotics,
K is for Keepers of lock-ups and prisons,
L is for Liquor, their friend in all seasons.

M is for Meanness rumsellers delight in,
N for the Noise, from brawling and fighting,
O the Opportunity we now are presenting,
P, Pledges to sign by drinkers repenting.

Q, the Queer People our pledges refusing,
R is for Reason, which tipplers are losing,
S for the Sermon each drunkard is preaching,
T for the Truth, which so many is reaching.

U for this Upas, so deadly, so blighting,
V is for Voters for temperance uniting,
W the Wisdom abstainers are gaining,
X the eXample from liquors abstaining,

Y for the Young in life's pleasant morning,
Z for the Zeal that gives them good warning,
& *saves them from drink*, the future adorning.

SHOT NO. 8.

A for *Alcohol*, which poisons man's brain,
  Destroying his sense, the very last grain;
  Those only are safe who always abstain,
  From drinks that make drunk, all men should refrain.

B stands for *Boys*, who frequent the place
  Where poisons are sold, producing disgrace;
  Which manhood and sense forever efface,
  And always have proved the foe of our race.

C for *Common Sense*, which says, "keep away
  From places where men are ruined for pay."
  When all men decide good sense to obey,
  From dram-selling shops they always will stay.

D for *Delusion*, the state of the mind,
  When, muddled by drink, man's reason is blind,
  Delusions, the worst we ever can find,
  Proceed from the drink destroying mankind.

E, Experience, by which *some must* learn
  From drinks that deceive forever to turn,
  When all are earnest the truth to discern,
  These drinks that defile; all people will spurn.

F stands for *Fraudulent* dealers in drink,
  Containing poison adapted to sink
  Good men into sots, *too tipsy to wink*,
  Too muddled in brain with reason to think.

G is for *Grasping* old landlords, who rent
  The place to sell drink, and get their per cent.,
  With hearts of *chilled steel*, too hard to relent,
  Remorseless as death, they seldom repent.

H is for *Hatred* of drinks that destroy,
  Which always is felt by every true boy,
  Such hatred of wrong produces true joy,
  And happiness brings, devoid of alloy.

I for *Injustice* this poison to sell,
  Which all that is good in man will expel,
  Compelling him oft in sorrow to dwell;
  Against drink so vile, mankind should rebel.

J is for *Joys* in homes of delight,
  Where none are controlled by base appetite,
  Where all are disposed to follow the right,
  For each others' good to always unite.

K, *King Alcohol*, a despot so vile
  As all of his dupes in sin to beguile;
  Man's body and soul, he'll surely defile,
  And, at his sad fate, *maliciously smile*.

L is for *Lads* unpolluted as yet;
  If they take to drink how deep the regret;
  If the pledge they keep, protection they'll get
  From joining at all the vile drunken set.

M for *Misery*, dealt out by the glass,
  In beer, cider, wine, and drinks of that class,
  This trade should be stopped, but we let it pass,
  That dealers in drink much wealth may amass.

N is for *Nonsense* to suffer a place
  To exist, which sells this liquid disgrace,
  When voters decide this truth to embrace,
  These dens will *all go*, not leaving a trace.

O is for *Order*, a law from on high
  With which all people may safely comply,
  These lovers of drink all order defy,
  And heaven's first law profanely deny.

P is for *Prudence*, which teaches us all
    From drinks to abstain, the mind that enthrall,
    That those who abstain ; through drink *never* fall ;
    That none can be safe when tasting at all.

Q is for *Quickness*, with which all should sign
    The pledge ; to abstain from brandy, and wine,
    And all other drinks to which they incline,
    That cause man's reason its seat to resign.

R is for *Reason*, which people should use,
    And not through vile drink, their nature abuse,
    No reason exists which men can excuse,
    Unless this poison they *always* refuse.

S stands for the *Strength* pure water will bring,
    When taken from well, lake, river, or spring,
    Dissolving our food ; to it we will cling,
    And thus, we'll be free from wine's bitter sting.

T for this *Traffic*—unholy, unjust,
    Increasing the sin, the crime, and the lust,
    A traffic the good must always distrust;
    We'll drive it from earth, for fight it we must.

U is for *Undone*—the wretch we behold
    Who once was possessed of thousands in gold ;
    Drink robbed him of all, before he was old,
    And left him to face starvation and cold.

V is for *Vagrant*, a burning disgrace
    To all of his friends, to all of his race ;
    Through all the wide earth he's no resting place,
    But will beg for drink the rest of his days.

W for *Wounds* which come " without cause,"
    By drinking of wine, defying God's laws ;
    If tippling at all, 'tis time now to pause,
    And angels above will shout their applause.

X stands for the *Cross;* on that we'll rely,
  And seek the true grace that comes from on **high**;
  Temptations to sin we then can defy,
  And trusting in God, his truth we will buy.

Y is for *Youth*, the time to enlist
  To live for the truth, all evil resist,
  To work for the right, the weak ones assist,
  Encouraging all from sin to desist.

Z stands for *Zeal*, which comes from on high,
  Impelling us all our talents to try,
  With faith in our God, on him to rely,
  The minions of sin to always defy.

& fighting for truth, united we'll stand,
  Extending our pledge throughout every land,
  Then freed from drink's curse, men's minds will **expand**,
  And temperance reign, majestic and grand.

Shot No. 9.

A for Appetite, created by wine,
B is for Beer, which all should decline;
C is for Cider, which kindles the blaze,
D the Drunkard it makes, who Satan obeys.

E for Excesses by drink brought about,
F is for Falsehoods, which liquor brings out;
G is for Gladness, which drinking dispels,
H is for Homes it changes to Hells.

I is for Influence, for good or for bad,
J is for " Jail-bird " by liquor made sad.
K is for Keenness of those who refuse,
L Liquor to buy, to sell, or to use.

M for Memory, which drinking destroys,
N is for No, the right word for our boys;
O is for Oaks, by water made strong,
P is for Poor-House, for drink's ragged throng.

Q is for Quack, who liquor prescribes,
R Ruining whom the poison imbibes;
S is our Standard, which always unfurled,
T Truth will promote, throughout all the world.

U is for Ungracious loafers and sots,
V Vile Victims of drink—no God in their thoughts;
W for Water the drink we should use,
X grades poison ales, which all should refuse.

Y stands for the Yoke of appetite strong,
Z for the Zeal which to us should belong,
& arm us with truth, to fight against wrong.

SHOT No. 10.

A is for Art of changing the grain,
Which nature creates, on hill, dale, and plain,
From the food which God intended for man,
To far the worst drink, since nature began.

B is for Brewer, the foe of his race,
Who seeks in God's grain, a means of disgrace;
He crushes it fine and rots out its life,
Changing it thus, to a demon of strife.

C stands for the Cash, which brewers receive
For making the drinks which always deceive;
And also for Crimes, the vilest and worst,
Committed by those by drunkenness cursed.

D for Distiller, who, seeking for wealth,
Spreads ruin, and shame, bad morals, ill-health ;
Poisons man's body, his mind, and his soul,
And leaves him a slave, in satan's control.

E is for Evils, too many to name,
Which flow down the stream of sorrow and shame;
That starts from the still, where satan presides,
And carries disgrace to happy firesides.

F is for Frolics, of Folly, and Fun,
Where lives of despair are often begun ;
And likewise for Fiends, who witness the scene,
And laugh with delight, that boys are so green.

G is for Graveyards—what horrors they tell
Of victims of rum, brought hither to dwell;
Whose lives were cut short by villainous drink,
And hastened by wine, down infamy's brink.

H is for Hardness of Heart, and of soul,
  Of all who submit to liquor's control,
  Heaping disgrace, on children and wife,
  And filling bright homes, with discord and strife.

I for Intemperance, our Nation's disgrace,
  Those only are safe, who never will taste
  Of drunkard's vile drink, é'er brewed or distilled;
  This army of sots, by tasting, is filled.

J is for Justice, enforced it will send
  Dram-sellers to jail—their victims defend ;
  Our duty to fight this traffic is plain,
  From drink that makes drunk, likewise to abstain.

K is for Kingdom of sin, shame, and woe,
  Which victims of drink are all sure to know ;
  Likewise for Kingdom, of virtue, and love,
  Enjoyed here below, continues above.

L is for Lamp-post ; so steady and sure,
  For those who enrich distiller and brewer ;
  Destroying their brains with virulent drink,
  Thus causing their homes, in ruin to sink.

M is for Mocker ; the scriptural name
  Of wine, which causes such sorrow and shame ;
  Likewise for Morals, which drinking dispels,
  Changing bright homes to lowest of hells.

N is for Newness of heart, and of life,
  For all who will leave drink's turmoil and strife,
  And look to their God, to give them the grace
  To spurn all the bad, and Jesus embrace.

O is for Outcasts, begotten by drink,
  By rum, they were tossed o'er infamy's brink ;
  From poison so vile, may all men abstain,
  For thus we only true safety can gain.

P is for Pledge, which wonderfully saves
    From vile drinking lives, from premature graves ;
    May people unite, the pledge to extend;
    Much evil, will thus be brought to an end.

Q is for Quarrels, which often commence
    When men in their drink, have lost their good sense ;
    The pledge let us take, from tasting keep clear,
    Then quarrels from drink no more will appear.

R for Rum-seller, who, seeking for wealth,
    Poisons his victims, in morals and health ;
    Does conscience object ? Cash brings the relief,
    Tho' blistered with tears, and cankered with grief.

S is for Shame, for Sadness, and Strife,
    The drunkard's queer choice through all his queer life;
    Likewise for Satan, who sits at his ease,
    Well pleased with the work in all the degrees.

T is for Torments, Transgressions, and Tears,
    This traffic has caused these thousands of years ;
    Likewise for Tempter, man's subtlest foe,
    Enticing him fast to regions below.

U for Unsoundness of those who still claim
    That any who drink are free from all blame ;
    Those sipping at all, a custom maintain
    From which none are safe, unless they abstain.

V is for Vineyard, where sunshine and rain,
    Produce the best fruit, mankind can obtain ;
    And also for Vat, where man rots the juice,
    And brings forth a drink, for satan's own use.

W for Water, all sparkling and bright,
    Which safely we drink, with purest delight ;
    It strengthens us all in muscle and brain,
    And fits us for work, a living to gain.

X brewers all use for branding the ale,
In numerous shops still offered for sale ;
From city, and town, we'll drive them away,
And thus hasten on the millenial day.

Y Yoke, that is easy—with burden so light
For all who enlist with Jesus to fight ;
And Yoke that is hard, for those who withstand
The light of these truths, throughout every land.

Z stands for Zeal, with which all will work,
Who living for truth no duty dare shirk ;
Believing in God, Christ's burdens they bear,
Till heaven they gain, his mansions to share.

& now may we all—our banners unfurled—
Go thunder these truths through all the wide world
Placing this traffic in fearful commotion,
Till abstinence reigns, from ocean to ocean.

SHOT No. 11.

A is for *Anguish*, that came to our world
When *Drink's tempting banner* at first was unfurled;
An anguish so *keen, so subtle and fine*
As *those only know*, who suffer through wine.

B is for *Blindness*, so sure to possess
All people, through wine, brought down to distress;
This poison in wine unsettles man's brain,
And robs him oftimes, of power to abstain.

C is for *Christians*, who all should maintain
This fight against drink, which poisons the brain;
Likewise, for *Curses*, which follow *all men*
Who tamper with wine, again, and again.

D for *Disgrace*, that *lurks* in the glass,
The tippler *don't see it*, and *swallows it fast*,
Likewise, for *Degrees*, by which he is changed
From a *man* to a *sot*, his nature deranged.

E for *Endeavor* the pledge to extend,
Enabling the *weak* their lives to amend;
And for *Entreaty*, which frequently saves
Those *smitten* by *drink;* from premature graves.

F is for *Firmness*, with which we should press
The *fight against* rum—humanity bless.
Likewise, for *Friendship*, which, *shown for the weak,*
Oft brings the results, which *true christians seek.*

G is for *Grandeur of the temperance work,*
Where *none* can afford their duty to shirk;
Likewise, for *Gutter*, from which we reclaim
Those sunk in *disgrace, in sorrow, and shame.*

H is for *Hopes* of a time that will come
  When *none* shall be cursed by the demon of rum,
  With *might*, may we work to hasten the time
  When *abstinence reigns, throughout every clime.*

I for *Improvement*, in body and soul,
  For all who break from this tyrant's control,
  Who *sever their chains*, and lead a new life,
  With peace, and content, for children and wife.

J is for *Jokes*, which often are true ;
  Don't joke the poor sot, *'tis unmanly in you ;*
  His *friends* deeply feel the burning disgrace,
  So save your *smart jokes* for some other place.

K is for *Knaves*, who liquor will sell,
  That *turns men to sots*, in anguish to dwell,
  Likewise, for *Keepers* of prisons and jails,
  Where those who sell drink—*their sins should bewail.*

L is for *License*—protecting the trade
  In poisons, *as vile as man ever made ;*
  For *license* men vote, *this traffic protect,*
  And *father this trade from satan direct.*

M is for *Madness*, and *Meanness* of men
  Who *change men to sots*, again and again,
  Furnishing liquor to poison their brains,
  Destroying their souls, while seeking their gains.

N is for *Nuisance*, the place where they sell
  The drink ; that entices men downward to dwell,
  May voters arise, and sweep them from earth,
  And speed them below, *where first they had birth.*

O is for *Outrage*, to let them remain,
  Still tempting to death—again, and again,
  If *man is afraid ;* let woman arise,
  For *she will succeed* wherever she tries.

P is for " *Prince of the Power of the Air,*"
Unwilling that we Christ's mansions should share ;
He *chuckles with glee when appetite strong,*
Unsettles man's brain, and makes him go wrong.

Q. Qualms, which *conscience* so often disturb,
The *publican's* soul can *seldom* perturb,
When *conscience* he heeds, he *leaves his vile trade ;*
And *drunkards* by him no longer are made.

R is for *Reasons,* which some try to give,
Enabling their trade still longer to live,
No reasons exist, not born down below,
Why business should live producing such woe.

S is for *Samples* of dram-seller's work,
All *bloated and vile,* each duty they shirk ;
Neglecting their wives and children at home,
To *ruin their lives* with villainous rum.

T is for *Treating,* a practice that leads
Our *finest young men to darkest of deeds ;*
By *treating,* men aid each other in sin,
While, *drinking alone,* but few would begin,

U is for *Urchins, for whom the heart bleeds,*
Smoking and chewing the *vilest of weeds,*
Whose parents *drink rum* and leave them at large,
To *early* become a *prison-house* charge.

V is for *Vices,* by tens and by scores,
Of him who heaven's wise teachings ignores ;
And for *Virtue* for each son and daughter,
Who seek for *true grace,* and stick to cold water.

W, the *Wonderful* change we behold
In all in the past by liquors controlled,
Who *now* are redeemed from drink's deadly power ;
With *manhood restored,* they're happy each hour.

X the *eXcuses* so many still make,
    That wine is required for the *"stomach's sake,"*
    While, if from *such stuff*, their stomachs were free,
    Their aches, and their pains, most surely would flee.

Y stands for *Years* of comfort and peace,
    For *all* who from *drink* will *sign their release ;*
    The pledges are here, *come quickly and sign,*
    These *drinks that destroy, forever resign.*

Z is for *Zeal*, which *wisely* displayed,
    Will drive from our midst this custom and trade,
    And *free us from all the evils*, that come
    From *selling*, and *drinking, nefarious rum.*

& may we all *work*, this cause to promote,
    By *pen*, and by *voice*, *example*, and *vote*,
    'Till *our entire race* from liquor is free,
    And *Temperance, reigns from mountain to sea.*

SHOT No. 12.

A is for Anguish, engendered by wine,
    By far the worst known in satan's design.

B is for Beer, which muddles the brain,
    We only are safe to always abstain,

C is for Cider, fermented, it brings
    Our boys to endure King Alcohol's stings.

D for Disturbance of nerve and of brain,
    For all who refuse from drink to abstain.

E is for Egg-nog, a drink that beguiles,
    Good men into sin—their nature defiles.

F for False teachings—with safety they claim
    These drinks can be used, which cause so much shame.

G is for Grog, which covers the list
    Of drinks that make drunk ; king satan assist.

H for High Hopes, of those who refuse
    Their lives to resign to liquor's vile use.

I for Intemperance, a world-wide disgrace,
    From which none are free, who frequently taste.

J is for Jolly young fellows who drink,
    Not knowing the depths to which they may sink.

K is for Keepers of rum-drinking holes,
    They ruin for gain, our bodies and souls.

L is for Lager, which often o'ercomes
    Man's reasoning powers, destroying bright homes.

M is for Music, so often in use
    Where lager is sold, to aid this abuse.

N is for Night, when music and dancing,
In lager saloons, sin's cause is advancing.

O is for Orgies held in such places,
From which wise boys, will turn their bright faces.

P is for Parents, whose teachings should save
Their children from drink, so sure to enslave.

Q for Quietness, which temperance brings
To all, who will drink from nature's pure springs.

R return ye sots, to water's embrace,
'Twill save you long years of burning disgrace.

S stands for Strength, which liquor destroys,
While water gives strength, increasing our joys

T is for Triumph of right, over wrong,
Our pledges assist to help it along.

U for Usefulness of all who in faith,
Will work against rum, while God gives them breath.

V for Vile Victims of alcohol's power,
Who deep in disgrace, so abjectly cower.

W for warnings that come from on high,
To "look not on wine," it's sting never try.

X stands for Cross, where Christ shed his blood
To free us from sin, and lead us to God.

Y stands for Youth, the season to sign
The pledge against drink, false pleasures resign.

Z is is for Zenith of virtue and grace,
Which all may obtain who water embrace.

& may we all work—this curse to remove,
Till called to abide in mansions above.

SHOT No. 13.

A is for Army of vile drinking sots,
Half a million strong; the very worst blots
To manhood's fair fame our race ever knew,
Who, ruined by drink, to Satan are true.

B is for the Boys, who often enlist
By tasting of wine; why won't they desist
When water so pure, so clear and so bright,
Will strengthen their brain, and give them delight?

C stands for Care, with which we should teach
Each child to abstain from poisons that reach
His brain, and his speech, his body, and soul,
Enchaining him fast—a slave to the bowl.

D is for Disease, Distress and Defeat,
Which those who use drink so surely will meet,
And for Disgrace, Disturbance, Disaster,
For all who drink will choose for their master.

E is for Effects, extensively felt
By all who to drink supinely have knelt,
Effects so alarming, distressing and base,
As drink only brings—mankind, to disgrace.

F is for Folly of those who will take
The glass to their lips, their reason to shake,
May all our bright boys this poison refuse,
And never, by drink their nature abuse.

G is for Greatness of mind and of soul,
Which comes not to those in liquor's control;
John the Baptist abstained, by God's written word,
And always was " Great, in sight of the Lord."

H is for Heights, to which we arrive
    In wisdom and truth—if rightly we strive;
    While if o'er our lives intemperance reigns,
    For wisdom and truth we've sin's guilty stains.

I is for Intellect, its seat is the brain,
    Which sober and clear, is reason's domain,
    But poisoned by wine it loses its seat,
    And man, soon becomes a drunkard complete.

J is for Jargon, as well as for Jails,
    Which always increase where drinking prevails,
    And also for Joys, which abstinence brings,
    Protecting us all from wine's smarting stings.

K is for Kindness, which shown for the weak,
    Often will cause them true wisdom to seek;
    Also for Keenness, with which we must move,
    As " wise as the serpent—as harmless as doves."

L is for Law, which based upon right,
    Will never to sin, the people invite,
    By licensing shops vile poison to sell,
    Which causes its slaves in horror to dwell.

M the Misery that drinking produces
    In poverty, crime, and other abuses;
    Without one feature, with power to redeem
    The men who sell drink, in public esteem.

N for Negligence, which causes our race,
    To tolerate shops of death and disgrace;
    May Nations awake and drive them below,
    Thus saving our earth much torment and woe.

O, Omnipotence, who only can know,
    The wretched despair, the sin and the woe,
    That drink has produced these ages of time,
    And nature abused throughout every clime.

P for "Perdition of ungodly men,"
So peopled by drink again and again,
And for Perversion of heaven's wise laws,
Of peopling perdition, so often the cause.

Q for Quantity of poison in drink,
Which causes its dupes in sorrow to sink;
And for Quality, which Satan desires
To poison man's brain, and kindle his fires.

R for Righteousness, Redemption and Rest,
For all who inherit a home with the blest;
Likewise for Ruin, which masters the brain
Of those who from drink, will seldom abstain.

S for the Sentence the Bible has passed
On all who will drink the poisonous glass;
In its sacred leaves we're told it will bring
The "poison of snakes, the adder's vile sting."

T stands for Truth, if once crushed to the earth,
Again it will rise, receive a new birth;
In grandeur and might, her cohorts advance,
• And raise men to life—God's glory enhance.

U is for Union; we all should unite
To crown with success this glorious fight;
And hasten the time when each son and daughter,
Is pledged to our cause, and sticks to cold water.

V is for views—so often all wrong,
Which cause men to taste, and join the vile throng;
These views we will change by logic and reason,
Wine's Votaries, save from nature's worst treason.

W for Wisdom, from God's holy book,
Which teaches, *from* wine for ever to look;
"Sorrow and babblings, contention and strife,"
Will thus be erased forever from life.

X for eXertion, our race to improve
By faith and hard work—by kindness and love ;
By Jesus inspired, the warfare we'll fight,
Assured of success of right, over might.

Y for Yesterday—'twill never return,
To-day is our own, new laurels to earn ;
Right onward we'll move, our cause to extend,
Thus serving our Lord, our Savior, and friend.

Z is for Zeal, which true workers all feel,
How much we possess our work will reveal ;
We'll watch, work and pray, till zeal from on high,
Enthuses our souls, brings victory nigh.

& now may we all forever abstain
From poisons, that steal our manhood and brain ;
And drink the pure water, by nature designed
As the only safe drink, to strengthen mankind.

SHOT No. 14.

A is for Antics by drinkers performed,
  Whose manhood, vile drink has sadly deformed;
  By kindness, these men oft-times, are reformed.

B is for Beer, which always contains
  The poison that steals man's wonderful brains,
  Polluting his soul with sin's guilty stains.

C is for Cider, where children begin
  The taste to acquire; then brandy and gin
  Step quick to the front, increasing the sin.

D for Delusion which drink brings to men;
  Also confusion, again and again,
  Pray let us abstain—we're free from it then.

E is for Egg-nog, a villainous drink,
  Which robs man of power correctly to think,
  And speeds him oft-times, down infamy's brink.

F is for Fellows who frequent the bar,
  Where men like poor fools, drink poisons that scar
  Their bodies and souls, their intellects mar.

G is for Grog-shop, King Satan's own place,
  From which, he sends forth both death, and disgrace,
  And often destroys the best of our race.

H is for Houses where publicans sell
  The drink, that prepares their victims for hell,
  And sends them below, in torment to dwell.

I for Industry, which keeps us away
  From places where souls are ruined for pay,
  Improving our homes, from day, unto day.

J stands for Jug, the tippler's dear chum
When filled full of beer, gin, whiskey or rum,
Which rob him of sense, of virtue, and home.

K is for Keenness of wit, and of sense,
Refusing these drinks on every pretence,
Saving character, health, and boundless expense.

L is for Landlord who rents the vile den,
Where men are engaged in poisoning men,
And souls are destroyed, again, and again.

M for "Man's inhumanity to man,"
Which, of all evils, now stands in the van,
But not down in God's original plan.

N is for Nature ; Her teachings will bring
The man in his thirst, to river or spring,
And make him avoid wine's venomous sting.

O for Obnoxious, a term that applies
To all who prefer the truth to despise,
Obeying, with ease, the father of lies.

P for Pandora, whose jar was unsealed,
When wine in his glory, at first took the field,
Causing good Noah to Satan to yield.

Q for Queer folks, who grumble and fret,
The worst ones to suit we ever have met,
Our cause is much cursed by this grumbling set.

R is for Reason, which, properly used
Has always, the drink of the drunkard refused,
And kept the man safe, from liquor's abuse.

S is for Strangeness of manner of life,
Of him who neglects his children and wife,
Sustaining saloons, with wickedness rife.

T for this Traffic, ungodly and vile,
Which man into sin can only beguile,
His body and soul so surely defile.

U for Unhappy, the state of the soul
Of all those held fast in Satan's control,
Sipping the poison in cup, glass, or bowl.

V is for Vampire, who sucks our life's blood,
By selling us that which does us no good,
While robbing us, both of clothing, and food.

W for Water, the drink that God brews,
In sunshine and cloud, in rains and in dews,
And gives to us all, with safety to use.

X stands for Cross—if to it we will cling,
'Twill furnish us drink from Heaven's own spring,
And while we exist—true happiness bring.

Y for the Yoke so many still bear,
Who stick to this cup of liquid despair,
King Alcohol's slaves ; his kingdom they share.

Z is for Zealous—the state of the mind
We all should maintain while tipplers so blind
Are changed into sots, disgracing mankind.

& zealously work these truths to extend,
The weak 'gainst the strong forever defend,
Till, blessed by our God, these vices shall end.

SHOT No. 15.

A for Abstinence from beer, cider, wine,
Which plain common sense says all should decline :
For liquors like these unbalance men's brains,
Polluting their souls with sin's guilty stains.

B for the Beauty of a temperance life,
Devoted to God, to children, and wife ;
Proclaiming the truth — relieving distress,
Devoted throughout the lowly to bless.

C the Charmed life teetotalers live,
By drinks that defile not ever deceived ;
Whose bodies are free from drink's deadly blight ;
With brains always clear, their reason is bright.

D for Decay, which changes the juice
Of fruits, to a drink for drunkards' own use ;
No drinks that make drunk, men's brains steal away,
Could ever exist except through decay.

E is for Error of tasting at all
Of drink that causes so many to fall ;
That changes good men to drunkards at length,
That weakness creates — and never gives strength.

F for the Folly that causes our race
To tolerate drink that brings such disgrace ;
No good e'er was known from drink to proceed,
While ruin and woe it hastens with speed.

G for the greenness of boys who don't fear
The cider to sip, the wine and the beer ;
From tipplers they change to loafers and sots,
Live vile, wretched lives, — humanity's blots.

H is for Habits extensively formed,
   By which many souls are sadly deformed ;
   The habits avoid that ruin your peace,
   Encouraged at all they swiftly increase.

I for Injunction that comes from on high,
   The wine-cup to shun, its taste never try ;
   A demon lurks there, and seeks for your soul,
   To rob it of peace ; its future — control.

J for Jelly-Fish, which well represents
   Those men we all know, who straddle the fence ;
   No bone in their backs, all sides they would please,
   They *float* all their lives, and change with each breeze.

K for the Keenness bright boys will possess,
   The habits to shun that breed such distress ;
   Bad habits forsake — don't keep them a day,
   They 'll hold you in sin, vile slaves without pay.

L is for Leader, which mortals all need,
   To follow through life, their soul's truly feed ;
   Jesus will lead us by wisdom and love,
   And tenderly feed us with food from above.

M stands for the Means that Christians should use,
   To spread the true light — men's minds disabuse ;
   By preaching, by vote, example and prayer,
   True Christians only their faith can declare.

N for Nice people: too nice for hard work,
   They worship the lily, the sunflower, and shirk
   The duties of life, so noble and grand,
   Which all of God's sons doth hold at command.

O for Obedience — all men should obey
   The law of their God ; from truth never stray ;
   When seeking God's will in his holy book,
   We read that on wine we never should look.

P for Penitence, which sinners must feel,
   Ere God in his grace his love can reveal ;
   And snatch them away from sin's mighty power,
   Enjoying his presence and love every hour.

Q for Quandary, in which the man's mind
   Not settled in truth so often we find ;
   By trusting in God the way is so clear
   That "wayfaring men" ne'er stumble nor fear.

R for Reprobates now ruined by rum,
   Who tipplers, then sots and loafers become,
   Their lives would you lead ? then cider and beer
   On which they commenced, please drink without fear.

S for Stumbling Blocks which Christians become,
   Who vote to license the traffic in rum ;
   Those voting by law this trade to uphold
   To God must account for sorrows untold.

T for Thankfulness that many enlist
   To live for the right, drink's power resist ;
   Our war is for life, to fight 'gainst the trade
   That loafers, and sots, and beggars has made.

U the Unguarded moments in life
   Which Satan seeks out to put in his knife ;
   We 'll watch, work, and pray, with Christ for our guide,
   And Satan no more with us can abide.

V the Vast army of people who drink,
   The van reaches o'er perdition's vile brink ;
   The rear passes on to the front with a will,
   Our boys then enlist, their places to fill.

W the Wonderful love of our God,
   Who in our pure hearts will make his abode
   If our sins we 'll forsake, and trust in his grace,
   Receiving through faith great comfort and peace.

X is a letter which always we find
   In exertion, example, and words out of mind,
   Which brewers have stolen to stamp the vile ale,
   To our world's deep disgrace, still offered for sale.

Y is for Youngsters just from their mammas,
   With pipes in their mouths, vile quids and cigars ;
   Which poison their blood and weaken their brains,
   Preparing their souls for Satan's domains.

Z for the Zest with which we should fight,
   This wrong to arrest — this evil to right ;
   Still trusting in God to help us o'ercome,
   With truth's mighty hand, this army of rum.

& working for God, our cause must succeed,
   And hearts crushed by rum no longer shall bleed;
   God's grace then shall reign where sin now abounds,
   'Till heavenly love our planet surrounds.